Poems that B U M P in the Night

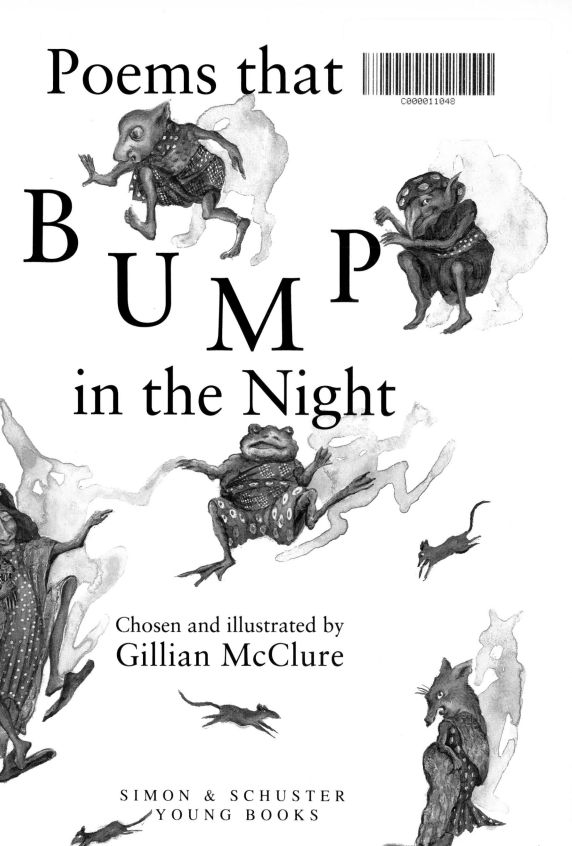

Chosen and illustrated by
Gillian McClure

SIMON & SCHUSTER
YOUNG BOOKS

For Paul

Acknowledgements

'Bully Night' copyright © Roger McGough from *Pie in the Sky* by Penguin Books reprinted by permission of Peters Fraser & Dunlop Group Ltd; 'Check' by James Stephens by permission of The Society of Authors on behalf of the copyright owner, Mrs Iris Wise; 'Let Us In' copyright © Olive Dove; 'The Magic Wood' copyright © Henry Treece by permission of John Johnson Ltd; 'Overheard on a Salt Marsh' copyright © Harold Monro by permission of Gerald Duckworth & Co Ltd; 'The Spunky' and 'Tom Bone' copyright © Charles Causley by permission of David Higham Associates; 'Storm in a Graveyard' copyright © Paul Coltman; 'Hist Wist' copyright © 1976 by the Trustees for the E. E. Cummings Trust reproduced with the permission of W. W. Norton & Co; 'Dare' copyright © Geoffrey Summerfield by permission of Scholastic Children's Books; 'Halloween' copyright © Leonard Clark from *Good Company* by permission of Dobson Books Ltd; 'The Two Old Women of Mumbling Hill' copyright © James Reeves from *The Wandering Moon and Other Poems* published by Puffin Books reprinted by permission of the James Reeves Estate; 'Things that go "bump" in the night' copyright © Spike Milligan; 'Nightening' copyright © Michael Dugan; 'Gentle Giant' copyright © Dennis Lee.

Every effort has been made to trace and contact copyright holders. The publishers will be pleased to make any necessary corrections in future printings, in the event of an error or omission in the use of copyright material.

First published in Great Britain in 1994
by Simon & Schuster Young Books
Campus 400, Maylands Avenue
Hemel Hempstead HP2 7EZ

Printed and bound in Belgium by Proost International Book Productions

British Library Cataloguing in Publication Data available

ISBN: 0 7500 1430 X
ISBN: 0 7500 1431 8 (pb)

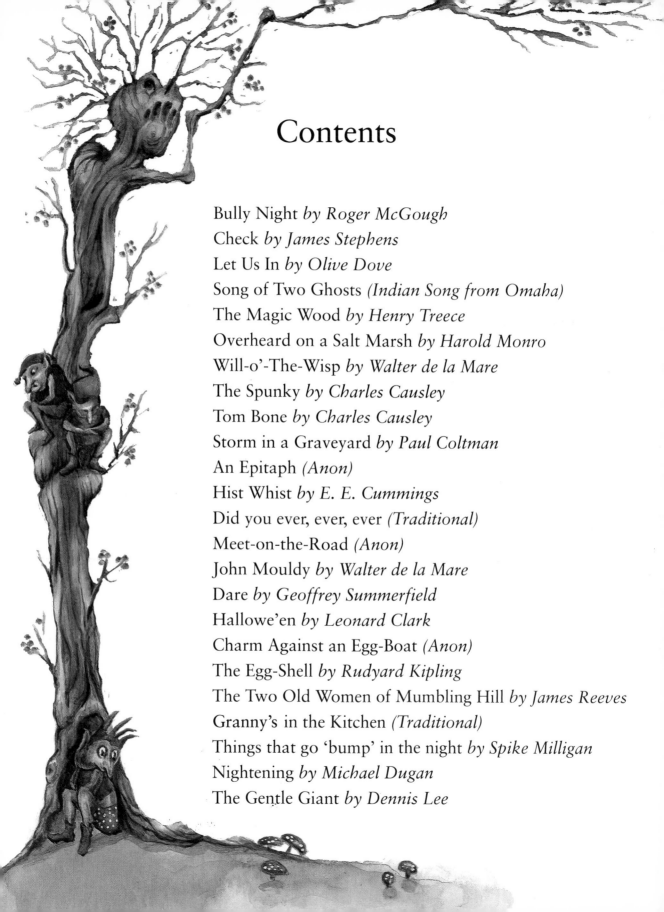

Contents

Bully Night

Bully night
I do not like
the company you keep
The burglars and the bogeymen
who slink
while others sleep

Bully night
I do not like
the noises that you make
The creaking and the shrieking
that keep me
fast awake.

Bully night
I do not like
the loneliness you bring
the loneliness you bring
The loneliness, the loneliness
the loneliness you bring,
the loneliness you bring
the loneliness, the

Roger McGough

Check

The Night was creeping on the ground!
She crept, and did not make a sound

Until she reached the tree: And then
She covered it, and stole again

Along the grass beside the wall!
- I heard the rustling of her shawl

As she threw blackness everywhere
Along the sky, the ground, the air,

And in the room where I was hid!
But, no matter what she did

To everything that was without,
She could not put my candle out!

So I stared at the Night! And she
Stared back solemnly at me!

James Stephens

Let Us In

'Let us in! Let us in!'
Who is crying above the wind's din?

'Let us in! Let us in!
We are pale and cold and thin.'

A clock chimes the midnight hour.
Are they creatures with magic power?

'Let us in! Let us in!
We are pale and cold and thin.'

They come and come and more and more
Close the curtains! Lock the door!

'Let us in! Let us in!
We are pale and cold and thin.'

'Let us in! Let us in!
We are pale and cold and thin.'

Olive Dove

Song of Two Ghosts

My friend
This is a wide world
We're travelling over
Walking on the moonlight.

Indian song from Omaha,
North America

The Magic Wood

The wood is full of shining eyes,
The wood is full of creeping feet,
The wood is full of tiny cries:
You must not go to the wood at night!

I met a man with eyes of glass
And a finger as curled as the wriggling worm,
And hair all red with rotting leaves,
And a stick that hissed like a summer snake.

He sang me a song in backwards words,
And drew me a dragon in the air.
I saw his teeth through the back of his head,
And a rat's eyes winking from his hair.

He made me a penny out of a stone,
And showed me the way to catch a lark
With a straw and a nut and a whispered word
And a pennorth of ginger wrapped up in a leaf.

He asked me my name, and where I lived;
I told him a name from my Book of Tales;
He asked me to come with him into the wood
And dance with the Kings from under the hills.

But I saw that his eyes were turning to fire;
I watched the nails grow on his wriggling hand;
And I said my prayers, all out in a rush,
And found myself safe on my father's land.

Oh, the wood is full of shining eyes,
The wood is full of creeping feet,
The wood is full of tiny cries:
You must not go to the wood at night!

Henry Treece

Will-o'-the-Wisp

Will-o'-the-Wisp
Come out of the fen,
And vex no more
Benighted men!
Pale, blue,
Wavering, wan,
'Will-o'-the-Wisp,
Begone, begone!'

But the trees weep,
The mist-drops hang,
Light dwindles
The bents among.
Oh, and he hovers,
Oh and he flies,
Will-o'-the-Wisp
With the baleful eyes.

Walter de la Mare

Overheard on a Saltmarsh

Nymph, nymph, what are your beads?
Green glass, goblin. Why do you stare at them?
Give them me.
                        No.
Give them me. Give them me.
                                    No.

Then I will howl all night in the reeds,
Lie in the mud and howl for them.
Goblin, why do you love them so?
They are better than stars or water,
Better than voices of winds that sing,
Better than any man's fair daughter,
Your green glass beads on a silver ring.
Hush, I stole them out of the moon.
Give me your beads, I desire them.
                                    No.

I will howl in a deep lagoon
For your green glass beads, I love them so.
Give them me. Give them me.
                              No.

Harold Monro

The Spunky *

The Spunky he went like a sad little flame,
All, all alone.
All out on the zogs and a-down the lane,
All, all alone.
A tinker came by that was full of ale,
And into the mud he went head over tail,
All, all alone.

A crotchety Farmer came riding by,
All, all alone.
He cursed him low and he cursed him high,
All, all alone.
The spunky he up and he led him astray,
The pony were foundered until it were day,
All, all alone.

There came an old Granny - she see the small Ghost,
All, all alone.
'Yew poor liddle soul all a-cold, a-lost,
All, all alone.
I'll give 'ee a criss-cross to save 'ee bide;
Be off to the Church and make merry inside,
All, all alone.

The Spunky he laughed, 'Here I'll galley no more!'
All, all alone.
And off he did wiver and in at the door,
All, all alone.
The souls they did sing for to end his pain,
There's no little Spunky a-down the lane,
All, all alone.

Anonymous

* *A spunky is a Will-o'-the-Wisp believed to be the*
wandering spirit of a still-born baby, or else of one who
has died before being christened. It was thought to beckon
passers-by towards the 'zogs' or marshes, because it wished to
be baptized with a a'criss-cross'. To 'galley' means to frighten and
to 'wiver' is to waver and quiver.

Tom Bone

My name is Tom Bone,
I live all alone
In a deep house on Winter Street.
    Through my mud wall
    The wolf-spiders crawl
    And the mole has his beat.

On my roof of green grass
All the day footsteps pass
In the heat and the cold,
    As snug in a bed
    With my name at its head
    One great secret I hold.

Tom Bone, when the owls rise
In the drifting night skies
Do you walk round about?
    All the solemn hours through
    I lie down just like you
    And sleep the night out.

Tom Bone, as you lie there
On your pillow of hair,
What grave thoughts do you keep?
    Tom says, Nonsense and stuff!
    You'll know soon enough.
    Sleep, darling, sleep.

Charles Causley

Storm in a Graveyard

When the great trees wag
and tug at their roots,
and the ground heaves,
tilting and rocking
tombstones and coffins,
then skulls nod,
boney fingers and feet
fidget and jig,
dancing

Paul Coltman

An Epitaph

Here lies John Bun;
He was killed by a gun.
His name was not Bun, but Wood;
But Wood would not rhyme with gun, but Bun would.

Hist Whist

hist whist
little ghostthings
tip-toe
twinkle-toe

little twitchy
witches and tingling
goblins
hob-a-nob   hob-a-nob

little hoppy happy
toad in tweeds
tweeds
little itchy mousies

with scuttling
eyes   rustle and run   and
hidehidehide
whisk

whisk   look out for the old woman
with the wart on her nose
what she'll do to yer
nobody knows

for she knows the devil   ooch
the devil   ouch
the devil
ach   the great

green
dancing
devil
devil

devil
devil

wheeEEE

E. E. Cummings

Did you ever, ever, ever

Did you ever, ever, ever,
In your leaf, loaf, life
See the deavil, doavil, devil
Kiss his weaf, soaf, wife?

No, I never, never, never
In my leaf, loaf, life
Saw the deavil, doavil, devil
Kiss his weaf, woaf, wife!

Traditional

Meet-on-the-Road

'Now, pray, where are you going?' said Meet-on-the-Road.
'To school, sir, to school, sir,' said Child-as-it-Stood.

'What have you in your basket, child?' said Meet-on-the-Road.
'My dinner, sir, my dinner, sir,' said Child-as-it-Stood.

'What have you for dinner, child?' said Meet-on-the-Road.
'Some pudding, sir, some pudding, sir,' said Child-as-it-Stood.

'Oh, then, I pray, give me a share,' said Meet-on-the-Road.
'I've little enough for myself, sir,' said Child-as-it-Stood.

'What have you got that cloak on for?' said Meet-on-the-Road.
'To keep the wind and cold from me,' said Child-as-it-Stood.

'I wish the wind would blow through you,' said Meet-on-the-Road.
'Oh, what a wish! What a wish!' said Child-as-it-Stood.

'Pray, what are those bells ringing for?' said Meet-on-the-Road.
'To ring bad spirits home again,' said Child-as-it-Stood.

'Oh, then I must be going, child!' said Meet-on-the-Road.
'So fare you well, so fare you well,' said Child-as-it-Stood.

Anon

John Mouldy

I spied John Mouldy in his cellar,
Deep down twenty steps of stone;
In the dusk he sat a-smiling,
    Smiling there alone.

He read no book, he snuffed no candle;
The rats ran in, the rats ran out;
And far and near, the drip of water
    Went whispering about.

The dusk was still, with dew a-falling,
I saw the Dog-star bleak and grim,
I saw a slim brown rat of Norway
    Creep over him.

I spied John Mouldy in his cellar,
Deep down twenty steps of stone;
In the dusk he sat a-smiling,
        Smiling there alone.

Walter de la Mare

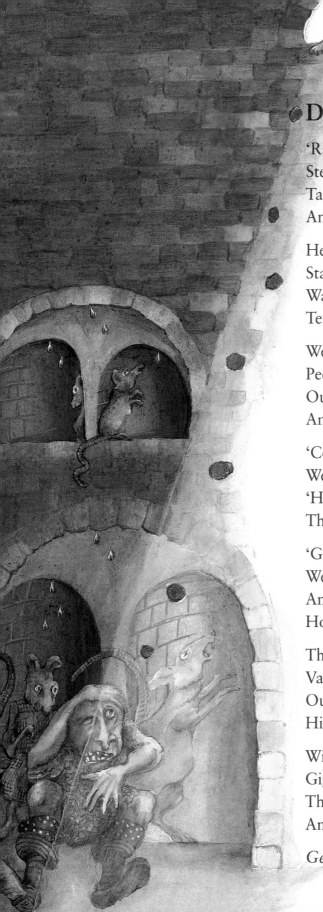

Dare

'Rawhead and Bloody Bones
Steals naughty children from their homes,
Takes them to his dirty den
And they are never seen again.'

He lurks at the bottom of the pit
Staring with one bloodshot eye,
Wallows in the sludge and slime,
Tempts us to venture close and pry.

We crawl right up to the very edge,
Peer into dripping pitch-dark mine.
Our fingers cling tight to the ledge
And shudders riot down my spine.

'Come out, old Rawhead, Bloody Bones!'
We heckle and bawl into the pit.
'Head!' 'Bones!' come echoing back,
Then, bolder still, we crouch and spit.

'Gob in your eye, old Bogeyman!'
We gather a heap of bricks and stones
And fling them fast and furious,
Hoping to hear his wounded groans.

Then, scattering to confuse his speed, -
Vamoose! - we run for dear life.
Our hackles rise, our ears burn,
His breath comes sharp as a butcher's knife.

Winded and shaken, we all flop down,
Giggling with terror and delight.
The cheerful sky fills our eyes,
And we bathe in a comforting sea of light.

Geoffrey Summerfield

Hallowe'en

This is the night when witches fly
On their whizzing broomsticks through the wintry sky;
Steering up the pathway where the stars are strewn,
They stretch skinny fingers to the waking moon.

This is the night when old wives tell
Strange and creepy stories, tales of charm and spell;
Peering at the pictures flaming in the fire
They wait for whispers from a ghostly choir.

This is the night when angels go
In and out of houses, winging o'er the snow;
Clearing out the demons from the countryside
They make it new and ready for Christmastide.

Leonard Clark

Charm Against an Egg-Boat

There's an old superstition that says that if you eat a boiled egg you must smash the shell up quickly to stop the witches stealing the unbroken shells, turning them into boats and rowing out to sea to brew up storms.

You must break the shell to bits, for fear
The witches should make it a boat, my dear:
For over the sea, away from home,
Far by night the witches roam.

Anon

The Egg-Shell

The wind took off with the sunset -
The fog came up with the tide,
When the Witch of the North took an Egg-shell
With a little Blue Devil inside.
'Sink,' she said, 'or swim,' she said,
And the Egg-shell went to sea.

The wind fell dead with the midnight -
The fog shut down like a sheet,
When the Witch of the North heard the Egg-shell
Feeling by hand for a fleet.
'Get!' she said, 'or you're gone,' she said,
But the little Blue Devil said 'No!'
'The sights are just coming on,' he said,
And he let the Whitehead go.

The wind got up with the morning -
The fog blew off with the rain,
When the Witch of the North saw the Egg-shell
And the little Blue Devil again.
'Did you swim?' she said. 'Did you sink' she said,
And the little Blue Devil replied:
'For myself I swam, but I *think*,' he said,
'There's somebody sinking outside.'

Rudyard Kipling

The Two Old Women of Mumbling Hill

The two old trees on Mumbling Hill,
They whisper and chatter and never keep still.
What do they say as they lean together
In rain or sunshine or windy weather?

There were two old women lived near the hill,
And they used to gossip as women will
Of friends and neighbours, houses and shops,
Weather and trouble and clothes and crops.

Then one sad winter they both took ill,
The two old women of Mumbling Hill.
They were bent and feeble and wasted away
And both of them died on the selfsame day.

Now the ghosts of the women of Mumbling Hill,
They started to call out loud and shrill,
'Where are the tales we used to tell,
And where is the talking we loved so well?'

Side by side stood the ghosts until
They both took root on Mumbling Hill;
And they turned to trees, and they slowly grew,
Summer and winter the long years through.

In the winter the bare boughs creaked and cried,
In summer the green leaves whispered and sighed;
And still they talk of fine and rain,
Storm and sunshine, comfort and pain.

The two old trees of Mumbling Hill,
They whisper and chatter and never keep still.
What do they say as they lean together
In rain or sunshine or windy weather?

James Reeves

Granny's in
the Kitchen

Granny's in the kitchen
Doing a bit of stitching
In came a bogeyman
And chased granny out
BOO!

'Well' says granny
'That's not fair'
'Well' says the bogeyman
'I don't care'

Traditional

Things that go 'bump' in the night

Things that go 'bump' in the night,
Should not really give one a fright.
It's the hole in the ear
That lets in the fear,
That, and the absence of light!

Spike Milligan

Nightening

When you wake up at night
And it's dark and frightening,
Climb out of bed
And turn on the lightening.

Michael Dugan

The Gentle Giant

Every night
At twelve o'clock,
The gentle giant
Takes a walk;
With a cry cried high
And a call called low,
The gentle giant
Walks below.

And as he walks
He cries, he calls:

'Bad men, boogie men,
Bully men, shoo!
No one in the neighbourhood
Is scared of you.
The children are asleep,
And the parents are too:
Bad men, boogie men,
Bully men, shoo!'

Dennis Lee